TALL TALES

Rainbow-walker
JOHNNY APPLESEED

Sky-bright Axe
PAUL BUNYAN

Coyote Cowboy
PECOS BILL

Pecos Bill Meets Paul Bunyan

HOUGHTON MIFFLIN COMPANY BOSTON

Atlanta Dallas Geneva, Illinois Palo Alto Princeton Toronto

Acknowledgments

"Sky-Bright Axe," "Coyote Cowboy," and "Rainbow Walker," from *American Tall Tales* by Adrien Stoutenburg. Copyright © 1966 by Adrien Stoutenburg. Reprinted by permission of Viking Penguin Inc.

"Pecos Bill Meets Paul Bunyan," from *Stories From Around the World,* edited by Marguerite Henry. Copyright © 1974 by Checkerboard Press, a division of Macmillan, Inc. Used by permission.

Text of "Backward Bill" from *A Light in the Attic:* Poems and Drawings by Shel Silverstein. Copyright © 1981 by Evil Eye Music, Inc. Reprinted by permission of Harper & Row, Publishers, Inc.

"When Paul Bunyan Was Ill" from *Back Packing* by Willie Reader. Copyright © 1975 by New Collage Press. Originally appeared in New Collage Magazine, Sarasota, Florida. Reprinted by permission of New Collage Press.

Credits

Cover illustration Phil Smith.

Illustration Shel Silverstein: pp. 82–83.
Lane Yerkes: pp. 10–11, 15, 18–19, 22, 28–29, 32–33, 36, 40–41, 43, 45, 46, 52–53, 56, 59, 60–61, 64–65, 67, 68, 74–75, 79.

Photography Johns Hopkins University Press: p. 84R.
AP/Wideworld Photos: pp.84L, 85.

Printed in the U.S.A.

ISBN: 0-395-45993-1

LMNOPQRST-D-9987654

TALL TALES

In the early days of the United States, most of the country was unsettled. Farmers in the East were beginning to move to the Midwest and beyond to find rich farmland. Lumberjacks in the thick forests of the North were cutting down trees to supply wood to build the new nation's towns and cities. Cowboys in the West were rounding up and herding beef cattle to market to feed the new nation's people.

As these pioneers worked and played, they told stories to entertain themselves and others. These stories were told and retold—and got funnier and crazier and wilder until they were pretty hard to believe. They had become tall tales.

Tall tales are American stories. They explain, in a crazy kind of way, how this country came to be what it is—as you'll see in these tall tales of three American folk heroes.

Table of Contents

Rainbow-walker

by Adrien Stoutenburg

Johnny Appleseed

No one has ever counted all the apple trees in America, but there are a lot of them. According to some people, we have all these apple orchards because a man called Johnny Appleseed (his real name was John Chapman) spent his life planting apple seeds. That was back in the days when most of our country was still a wilderness.

Johnny Appleseed loved apple trees more than almost anything else. He loved animals, too; some say he could talk to them. When he was still a small boy in Boston, people brought hurt or sick animals to him. Johnny had a kind of magic in his hands that helped him to heal hurt creatures, just as it helped him to grow trees and plants.

One day, when Johnny was a young man, a stranger came by Johnny's house. Johnny was picking apples from the ground, where the wind had blown them.

The man stopped and said, "I haven't seen apples like that in two years."

"Where have you been?" Johnny asked him.

"Working on a flatboat out west in the Indian country.

There aren't any apple trees growing out there. I'd like to buy a sack of your apples. Maybe they'll keep long enough for my wife and children back in the Ohio Territory to enjoy them."

Johnny fixed up a sackful. "I don't want any money," he said. "Just save the seeds when you get home, and plant them."

"That's a good idea, young fellow," the man said. "Thanks."

Johnny sat down under one of the apple trees and thought about what the man had said. Many families were moving west. If they carried apple seeds with them and planted them, there would be orchards sprouting up all over. Johnny knew his own orchard wasn't large enough to provide all the seeds needed. And there weren't as many settlers starting out from Boston as from a place like Pittsburgh, which was farther west.

Johnny thought a long time. Then he began gathering all the apple seeds from the apples on the ground. Before long, he had a small leather sack full of seeds.

A house sparrow flew down to pick up one of the seeds which had fallen from the sack.

"You leave that seed be, Mrs. Sparrow," Johnny said. "That's going to be an apple tree."

Two small boys going by heard him. "There's that loony Johnny, talking to himself again," one said.

"My folks say he's light in the head," the other said.

Johnny heard them and laughed, rolling a firm, red apple in his hands. He did not care what people said.

The next day, Johnny put the sackful of seeds over his shoulder and a small bundle of food in his pocket and started walking toward Pittsburgh. The dust spurted up in small clouds behind his bare heels. The wind made his long, black hair stand out behind his ears. Off in the distance, in the direction he was going, a rainbow shone in the sky, pink and yellow, green and blue. To Johnny the pink was the color of apple blossoms, and the pale green was the color of apples before they were ripe.

It took Johnny quite a long while to reach Pittsburgh. When he got there, he worked until he had enough money to buy a piece of ground. Then he started planting an apple orchard. Before long, apple trees were sprouting up around him like grass. As soon as the trees were large enough to bear fruit, Johnny gathered the seeds.

Whenever the people traveling west stopped to ask Johnny for food or water or a place to rest, he gave them apple seeds as well. And he never took any money.

"That's no way to run a business," some of the travelers said.

Johnny laughed. "I like giving orchards away."

People said, "That Johnny Appleseed is crazy."

Johnny kept on giving away sackfuls of seeds. He gave them to farmers and hunters, trappers and boatmen, soldiers and settlers. One day, he realized that he would have to find more seeds than his orchard could produce. He knew that all around Pennsylvania in the fall people put apples into wooden presses. They squashed and squeezed the apples to get out the bubbling juice for apple cider. And they threw the bright brown seeds away.

"I'm going to go out and get all those wasted seeds," Johnny said to a squirrel he had tamed.

The squirrel waved its tail and said, "Ch-kk, ch-kk," which to Johnny sounded like, "Go ahead."

Johnny put on his hat. It was a strange hat, for it was a kettle turned upside down. But it was more than a hat. It was something handy to cook in, if he stopped by the side of the road and wanted hot food. He looked around for some good traveling clothes. Everything he had was in rags. He saw a pile of gunny sacks which he used for gathering apples. He picked out the longest sack, cut holes in it for his head and arms, and put it on. Nobody could want a better traveling suit, thought Johnny.

Johnny Appleseed went walking up and down and back and forth across Pennsylvania. The Dutch farmers let him have the apple mash from their cider presses. Then, all winter long, Johnny picked out the seeds and dried them. In the spring, he gave the seeds away to anyone who stopped on his way west.

Sometimes, when settlers came back from the western territories, Johnny would ask, "Did you plant the seeds I gave you?"

Often, a settler would answer, "Oh, I forgot."

So, Johnny decided to go west himself and plant his own orchards. He rigged up a boat by lashing two canoes together, loaded them full of apple seeds, and set off down the Ohio River.

That was the only time Johnny used a boat. From then on he walked, hundreds and thousands of miles, carrying apple seeds with him. Most of the time he went barefoot, tramping through rain and snow. Wherever settlers gave him a small piece of land, he planted his orchards. Soon there were apple trees growing along the creeks and rivers all over Ohio and Indiana.

It was hard work, but Johnny did not think of it as work. It was what he wanted to do. Every time a sapling burst into bloom, he forgot about his tired feet and the iron kettle hat bumping his forehead. He slept out in the open most of the time, with only the sky for a cover and a fox or raccoon curled up beside him to help keep him

warm. When it snowed or rained, he slept in a settler's barn. And sometimes he stayed with Indians.

Johnny had many Indian friends, even though most Indians in those days hated the white men, who were taking over their land.

"Johnny Appleseed is crazy," some of the white men said.

"He is a powerful medicine man," most of the Indians said. "He heals the sick babies and warriors. He makes good medicine from the plants, and he talks to the animals."

Often, Johnny walked through areas where there were neither kindly settlers nor Indians. One bitterly cold night, the only shelter he could find was a large, hollow log. Johnny crawled into the log. He had gone only a few feet when he bumped into something big and soft, and he heard a sleepy, growling noise. It was dark inside the log, but Johnny could make out two eyes looking at him. The eyes belonged to a bear who had decided the log would make a fine bedroom for his winter's sleep.

Johnny calmly said, "Excuse me, Brother Bear," and crawled back out.

On another time, in the late summer, Johnny was resting at the end of the day. He had built a fire to heat up some cornmeal mush in his kettle hat. Suddenly, Johnny noticed that the air was full of flying sparks. The sparks headed toward the fire instead of shooting up from it as actual sparks would do. He looked closer and saw the sparks were tiny, buzzing insects. The insects were blinded by the flames and flew into the fire, where they burned.

Johnny jumped up and put out his fire, even though the cornmeal had not yet cooked. It was better to eat cold food, thought Johnny, than to have any living thing die because of his fire.

There are many tales about Johnny's traveling through the forests without any fear of wild animals. One of the stories people tell is about Johnny and a wolf.

One day, Johnny was busy gathering certain plants, called herbs, which were useful in curing sick people and animals. He was picking some wild ginger, when he heard a long, whimpering howl.

Johnny turned and saw a large black wolf. The wolf saw Johnny, too, and snarled, but it did not move. Johnny walked toward the animal, saying, "I am a friend, Brother Wolf."

The wolf snarled again, and then Johnny saw that its foot was caught in a steel trap.

"Poor beast," Johnny said. He bent down and worked open the jaws of the trap. "Now you are free," he told the wolf.

The wolf hopped back a step and then fell. The leg which had been caught in the trap was bleeding.

Johnny reached out and stroked the wolf's dark, sharp ears. The wolf showed its teeth.

"Don't be afraid," Johnny said. He took a pack from his shoulders, drew out some cloth strips, and bandaged the wolf's leg. When he was through, the wolf licked Johnny's wrist.

It took several days for the wolf's leg to heal. Johnny Appleseed stayed with the animal and took care of it. He fed the wolf and brought it water in his metal hat. When the wolf was well, Johnny started off on his travels again, his seed packs swinging in time with his step.

He had walked only about a hundred feet when he

heard something padding along behind him. It was the black wolf.

From then on, wherever Johnny went, the wolf followed. At night, they slept together under the stars, or huddled in a cave together, out of the rain. By day, they went from cabin to cabin, and some say the great wolf would dig holes with his paws for Johnny's apple seeds.

Johnny began to carry other things besides seeds. He put small gifts into the bags swinging from his shoulders—dolls he had whittled out of wood, pieces of bright cloth or ribbons, pretty speckled stones he had found, or berries to put on a string for a necklace. He gave most of these things to the settlers' children.

Johnny's eyes stayed as bright as ever, even though his dark hair began to turn gray. The black wolf that traveled with him grew old like Johnny, and the wolf's eyes grew dim. The wolf trotted close at Johnny's heels, for that was

the only way it could keep on the path. People say that because Johnny loved all wild creatures so much, the wolf learned to love them too. Rabbits would come and drink from the same pool where the wolf drank. Birds would ride on Brother Wolf's shoulder. Even the settlers, who distrusted wolves, learned to like Johnny's wolf.

But one night, a farmer who was new to the frontier saw the huge wolf near his chicken yard. The farmer put his shotgun against his shoulder and aimed.

Johnny Appleseed cried out to stop the farmer, but it was too late. The gun thundered, and the pet wolf leaped into the air as the shot hit its heart. The wolf fell back to earth and lay still.

Johnny sat for a long while beside his dead companion, stroking the thick fur. He looked up into the sky, seeking some brightness to drive away the gray sorrow he felt. But the sky was clouded over, without stars.

Johnny dug a grave for Brother Wolf by the side of a creek. After he had covered his old, faithful friend with soft earth, he reached into his pouch of apple seeds. He found the brightest, smoothest seeds of all, and carefully planted them around the grave.

Today, people say the spot is filled with apple trees with trunks as big as the legs of elephants. And they say that in spring the blossoms are so thick, a bee can scarcely fly between them.

After the wolf died, Johnny went on alone, still giving away apple seeds, and still planting orchards. The owls followed him at night, and even the shy deer would come out to meet him on the woodland trails at morning. But none stayed with him night and day, as the gentle black wolf had done.

Even though he felt lonely, Johnny was happy. Wherever he stopped, he handed out his seeds and preached about the beauty of things. He also preached about the need for kindness, especially kindness to animals. When settlers had horses too old to work any more, or too lame to be of use, they sometimes turned these horses out into the woods to die. When Johnny came across these animals, he took care of them and found them new homes.

He went on and on in his ragged clothes and his clanging hat, planting trees. Everywhere he went orchards sprang up. Where only weeds or brush had been, there was cloud on cloud of apple blossoms.

"He's loony, that Johnny Appleseed," some people said.

"He's lightheaded, that's certain," others agreed.

Johnny laughed, for he did not care what people said. He walked on, his bare heels kicking the leaves aside, until one day he was too tired to walk any farther.

On that day, he crawled into a small orchard near Fort Wayne, Indiana. He put one of his seed pouches under his head for a pillow. He lay there, looking up at the waving branches of apple trees and at the blue sky shining beyond.

Johnny Appleseed closed his eyes, listening to the leaves clapping together overhead. The sound faded, and the world turned dark. Then, suddenly, Johnny heard a soft whining. He thought he saw Brother Wolf standing beside him, his pink tongue hanging out as if he had traveled a long, long way. And there, hopping about among the tree roots, was Mrs. Sparrow. There, too, was the big, sleepy bear Johnny had met years before in the round darkness of a hollow log. And creeping out of the orchard shadows came raccoons and foxes, bobolinks and hummingbirds, shy deer, and lame, blinking horses.

Johnny sat up, rubbing his eyes. He looked at the sky again. Shimmering in the air, like a bridge of braided flowers, was a rainbow.

Johnny Appleseed leaped to his feet. He picked up all of his seed pouches and slung them over his shoulder. Then he called to the animals, "Brother Wolf, Sister Sparrow, Brother Bear . . ."

He started up the rainbow. The animals and the birds followed. Brother Wolf was the first, tagging at Johnny Appleseed's heels. Two orioles rode on the wolf's shoulders.

When they all reached the top of the rainbow, Johnny began throwing apple seeds all over the sky. If they stuck in the sky, they would grow into stars. If they fell to earth, they would become trees. Johnny looked down at the land covered with orchards and knew his work was done.

The next morning, a traveler going westward paused by the apple orchard where Johnny had stopped to rest. Under the brightest tree of all lay the small body of Johnny Appleseed, still dressed in a gunny sack and still wearing

his strange kettle hat. All around him, sitting in a quiet circle, were wild animals.

The traveler started on his way, planning to tell the nearest settler of what he had found. Then he saw three bright brown apple seeds lying at his feet. He picked them up and took them with him, wondering where he should plant them.

That is what some people say. Judging by all the apple trees there are, east and west, north and south, it seems someone must have carried on the planting Johnny Appleseed began.

Discussion

1. Most people think Johnny Appleseed is crazy. Is he? Support your answer.

2. Johnny doesn't care what other people think of him. Is that a good or a bad thing? Support your answer.

3. Which parts of this tall tale might actually be true? Which parts are clearly make-believe? Which parts might be either? Support your answer.

Sky-bright Axe

Sky-bright Axe

by Adrien Stoutenburg

Paul Bunyan

Some people say that Paul Bunyan wasn't much taller than an ordinary house. Others say he must have been a lot taller to do all the things he did, like sticking trees into his pockets and blowing birds out of the air when he sneezed. Even when he was a baby, up in Maine, he was so big he knocked down a mile of trees just by rolling over in his sleep.

Everyone was nervous about what might happen when Baby Paul grew older and started crawling. Maine wouldn't have any forests left.

Paul's father, who was an ordinary-sized man, was a bit nervous about it all himself. One night he had wakened to find his bed down on the floor. There beside it sat Baby Paul, a crosscut saw in one hand. In the other hand he held one of the sawed-off legs of the bed. He was chewing on it to help his teeth grow.

"I'll have to put him somewhere safe," Paul's father decided, "where he won't be a public nuisance."

He cut down some tall trees growing near his own cabin and built a boat shaped like a cradle. Paul's mother tucked Paul into it. Then Paul's parents put a long rope on the floating cradle and let it drift out to sea a little way.

It was a lovely, blue-green place for a cradle, with fish flashing around and the waves making small, humpbacked motions underneath. Baby Paul sucked his thumb and watched the seagulls flying over, light shaking from beneath their wings. Paul smiled, and then he hiccoughed. The hiccough started a gale that nearly blew a fishing boat all the way to the North Pole.

Finally, Paul went to sleep. He snored so loudly the gulls went flapping toward land for they thought a thunderstorm was coming. Then young Paul had a bad dream, brought on by the extra-large ham his mother had given him for breakfast. He tossed about in his sleep and started the cradle rocking. Each time the cradle rocked it sent a wave as big as a building toward shore. Paul tossed harder, and the waves grew even larger, bigger than cities. They smashed against the shore and threatened to drown everything on land.

People scampered up church steeples. They scrambled onto roof tops. They clawed their way up into trees, and they yelled for the government to save them. The settlers for miles around put rifles on their shoulders and marched up to Paul's father.

"Get that baby out of here!" they shouted. "He's a danger to the whole state. A baby like that is against the Constitution!"

Paul's father, and his mother, too, couldn't help feeling a bit proud of how strong Paul was. But they knew that the smartest thing to do was to move away. No one seems to know exactly where they went. Wherever it was, Paul didn't cause too much trouble for the rest of the time he was growing up. His father taught him certain things which helped.

"Don't lean too hard against smallish trees or buildings, Son," his father told him. "And if there are towns or farmers' fields in your way, step around them."

And Paul's mother told him, "Never pick on anybody who isn't your own size, Son."

Since there wasn't anyone his size around, Paul never got into fights. Being taller than other boys, by about fifty feet or so, he was naturally the best hunter, fisherman, walker, runner, yeller, or mountain climber there was. And he was best of all at cutting down trees and turning them into lumber. In those days, when America was new, people had to cut down a lot of trees. They needed the lumber for houses, churches, town halls, ships, bridges, ballrooms, stores, pencils, wagons, and flag poles. Luckily, the trees were there, stretching in tall, wind-shining rows across America. The trees marched up mountains and down again. They followed rivers and creeks. They massed up together in purple canyons and shoved each other out of the way on the shores of lakes. They pushed their dark roots down into rock and their glossy branches into the clouds.

Paul liked to flash a sky-bright axe over his head. He loved the smell of wood when it was cut and the look of its sap gleaming like honey. He didn't chop trees down in any ordinary way. With four strokes he would lop all the limbs and bark off a tree, making it a tall, square post. After he had squared up miles of forest in a half-hour, he would take an axe head and tie a long rope to it. Then he would stand straddle-legged and swing the axe in a wide circle, yelling, "T-I-M-B-E-R-R-R-R! Look out!" With every swing and every yell, a hundred trees would come whooshing down.

The fallen trees had to be hauled down to a river so that they could be floated to a sawmill. Paul grew a bit tired of lugging bundles of trees under his arms, and he wished he had a strong friend to help him. Also, at times he felt lonely, not having anyone his size around.

About the time he was feeling loneliest, there came the Winter of the Blue Snow. Paul, who was full-grown by then, had never seen anything like the blue flakes falling from the sky. Nobody else had either, and perhaps they never will, unless it happens again. The blue snow fell softly at first, like bits of sky drifting down. The wind rose and the flakes grew thicker. The blue snow kept falling, day after day. It covered branches and roof tops, hill and valley, with blue, and Paul thought it was about as beautiful a sight as anyone could want.

One day when Paul was out walking in the blue snow, he stumbled over something the size of a mountain. The mountain made a faint mooing sound and shuddered.

"Excuse me," said Paul and looked closer.

Two huge, hairy ears stuck up above the snowdrift. The ears were as blue as the snow.

"Who are you?" Paul asked. There was no answer. Paul grabbed both of the ears and pulled.

Out of the snow came a shivering, clumsy, completely blue baby ox. Even its round, blinking eyes and its tail were blue. Only its shiny nose was black. The calf was the largest Paul had ever seen. Strong as he was, he felt his muscles shake under the creature's weight.

"Ah! Beautiful blue baby!" Paul said. He cradled the half-frozen calf in his great arms and carried it home. There he wrapped the baby ox in warm blankets and sat up all night taking care of it. The calf did not show much

sign of life until morning. Then, as the dawn light came through the window, the ox calf stood up. The calf stretched its neck out and sloshed its wet tongue lovingly against Paul's neck.

Paul gave a roar of laughter, for his one ticklish spot was his neck.

Paul patted the baby ox and scratched his silky, blue ears. "We will be wonderful friends, eh Babe? You will be a giant of an ox and carry forests for me on your back."

That is how it happened that Babe the Blue Ox went with Paul Bunyan when Paul started out into the world to do his mighty logging work. By that time, Babe had his full growth. People never could figure out how long Babe was. They had to use field glasses even to see from one end of Babe to the other. And there were no scales large enough to weigh Babe. Paul did measure the distance between Babe's eyes, and that was exactly forty-two axe handle lengths and one plug of tobacco. Every time Babe needed new iron shoes for his hoofs, a fresh iron mine had to be opened. The shoes were so heavy that a man couldn't carry one without sinking up to his knees in solid rock.

Paul and the Blue Ox logged all over the northern timber country, from Maine to Michigan, Wisconsin, and Minnesota. Paul hired many men to help him. These lumberjacks liked working for Paul Bunyan, because he was always good to them and made sure that they had plenty of food.

The lumber crews liked pancakes best, but they would gobble up and slurp down the pancakes so fast that the camp cooks couldn't keep up with them, even when the cooks got up twenty-six hours before daylight. The main problem was that the griddles the cooks used for frying the pancakes were too small.

The winter that Paul was logging on the Big Onion River in Michigan, he decided that he had to do something about making a big enough griddle. He went down to the plow works at Moline, Illinois, and said, "I want you fellows here to make me a griddle so big I won't be able to see across it on a foggy day."

The men set to work. When they were finished, they had built a griddle so huge there was no train or wagon large enough to carry it.

"Let me think what to do," said Paul. "We'll have to turn the griddle up on end, like a silver dollar, and roll it up to Michigan." He hitched the Blue Ox to the upturned griddle, and away they went. It wasn't any job at all for Babe and Paul, though they had to hike a couple of hundred miles. A few miles from the Big Onion lumber camp, Paul unhitched Babe and let the griddle roll on by itself. When it stopped rolling, it started to spin as a penny does when it's ready to fall. It spun around and around and dug a deep hole in the ground before it flopped down like a cover over the hole.

The lumberjacks cheered and rushed off to haul a few acres of trees into the hole for a fire. The cook and a hundred and one helpers mixed tons of batter. When everything was ready, with the flames under the griddle blazing like a forest fire, Paul picked out a crew of men who could stand the heat better than others. He had them strap fat, juicy slabs of bacon on their feet.

"You men skate around on that griddle and that'll keep it well-greased," he told them.

The men skated until the griddle shone with bacon fat.

White batter came pouring out onto the griddle and soon the smell of crisp, brown, steaming pancakes was drifting across the whole state. There were tons of pancakes—with plenty left over for Babe, who could eat a carload in one gulp.

There wasn't much Paul couldn't do, especially with Babe's help. But there was one job that seemed almost too hard even for him. That was in Wisconsin, on the St. Croix River. The logging road there was so crooked, it couldn't find its own way through the timber. It would start out in one direction, then turn around and go every which way until it grew so snarled up it didn't know its beginning from its end. The teamsters hauling logs over it would start home for camp and meet themselves coming back.

Maybe even Babe couldn't pull the kinks and curves out of a road as crooked as that one, Paul thought, but there was nothing to do but try.

He gave Babe several extra pats as he put the Blue Ox's pulling harness on. Then he hitched Babe to the end of the road and stood back.

Babe lowered his head and pushed his hoofs into the earth. His muscles stood out like rows of blue hills. He strained forward, pulling at the road. He stretched so hard that his hind legs spraddled out until his belly nearly scraped the ground. The road just lay there, stubborn as could be.

"You can do it, my big beautiful Babe!" Paul said.

Babe tried again. He strained so hard that his eyes nearly turned pink. He sweated so that water poured from the tips of his horns. He grunted and pulled, and his legs sank into the ground like mighty blue posts.

There was a snap, and then a loud C-R-A-C-K! Paul saw

the first kink come out of the road, and he cheered. The road kept fighting back, flopping around and trying to hold on to its crooked twists and turns, but it was no match for Babe. At last, the road gave a kind of shiver and then lay still. Babe pulled it straighter than a railroad tie.

Paul Bunyan's chest swelled up so with pride that it broke one of his suspenders. The broken suspender whizzed up into the sky like a long rubber band. Just then, thousands of wild ducks were flying overhead. The suspender wrapped itself around the ducks and strangled the whole flock. Paul felt sorry for the ducks, but there was nothing to do but gather them up and hand them over to the cooks.

That night, after a wonderful duck dinner, Paul's bookkeeper John Inkslinger started writing down all that had happened. He was busily scratching away with his pen when he saw that he had only two barrels of ink left. He asked Paul what to do.

"That's easy," said Paul. "Don't bother to dot your *i*'s or cross your *t*'s. You'll save enough ink that way to get by until we can haul in another load of ink in the spring. Then you can fix up the *i*'s and *t*'s."

Winters could be very cold there in Wisconsin and Minnesota. One year, Lake Superior froze solid from top to bottom. In the spring, Paul had to haul all the ice out of the lake and stack it up on shore to thaw.

That same winter, men's words froze in front of their mouths and hung stiff in the air. Brimstone Bill, who was a great talker, was frozen in by a solid wall of words all turned to ice. Paul had to chip the ice from around Bill's shoulders, tie a rope to him, and have Babe pull him out.

The greatest logging job Paul ever did was in North Dakota, where some of the trees were so tall it took a man a whole day to see up to their tops. Shortly after Paul had finished logging off most of the white pine, spruce, and hemlock in Minnesota, he received a letter from the King of Sweden. Paul's Swedish blacksmith Ole read the letter to Paul.

"The king says there are too many Swedes in Sweden. He wants to send a batch of them over here, but they need rich farmland without many trees, so they can raise wheat. He says he'll pay you in silver and gold if you can fix up a place for them."

Paul thought awhile, puffing on his pipe so hard that the sky began to cloud over. "North Dakota's the place," he said. "Nice and flat for farming. I'll fix it up for the Swedes, but I'm going to have to build the biggest logging camp ever built."

There never was such building, banging, tree-whacking, and hammering as went on in North Dakota when Paul started the new camp. Cook houses, bunk houses, and sheds grew up out of the ground, each building as big as a good-sized town. The dining room alone was so long that the man who brought the salt and pepper wagons around started out at one end in the morning and did not reach the other end until night.

Paul had found that it was easier to skid logs on roads made slippery with ice. There weren't many lakes in North Dakota, so Paul hauled his water for freezing from Lake Superior. He put the water into a big tank which Babe pulled. The thousands of lakes in Minnesota today were made by Babe's hoofs sinking into the ground and the holes filling up with water that leaked out of the tank. On one trip, Babe slipped and the tank tipped over. All the water ran out and started the Mississippi River.

On the day that Paul had cut down the last big tree in

North Dakota, he stood looking around proudly. Then he frowned. Everywhere he looked there were hundreds and thousands of stumps sticking up. The Swedish farmers weren't going to like those stumps standing in the way of their plows.

"Blast it all!" Paul said, angry at himself for not having pulled the trees up roots and all. "Blast!" he thundered again and brought his fist whistling down on the stump beside him. The stump sank a foot below ground.

Paul Bunyan stared, scratched the side of his head, and stomped off to find Ole the blacksmith. "Ole," said Paul, "I want you to make me a maul—and make it as strong as Brimstone Bill's breath!"

The next morning, before the regular workday began, Paul went out with the new maul, which was like a giant hammer. He began knocking the stumps down into the ground. After about two weeks, working a couple of hours each morning, he had hammered every stump into the earth.

The King of Sweden was pleased when he heard about the fine job Paul had done, but one thing troubled him. He sent the Swedish ambassador to ask Paul if the soil in North Dakota was rich enough to grow fine crops.

"I'll prove that it is," said Paul. He got himself a kernel of corn, dug a hole four feet deep with a flick of his thumb, and dropped the corn in. "You come back in a week," he told the king's messenger, "and you'll see a fat stalk of corn pushing up out of the ground." He started to walk off, when he heard a rustling, whooshing sound behind him.

Paul turned. The kernel of corn had already sprouted and was rising up like a green rocket. In one minute it grew as high as Paul Bunyan's eyebrows. In two minutes more its tip struck a flying eagle and then split a cloud in two.

The Swedish ambassador's false teeth jumped out of his mouth and started biting the ground in excitement. "You'd better stop that corn growing!" he yelled at Paul. "It's apt to poke a hole in the sky and let all the air out. Besides, if I tell the king about it, he'll think it's just a tall story I made up."

Paul called to his men. "Ole," he said when all the men arrived, "you climb up there fast and cut the top off."

Ole straddled the stalk, but the thing was growing so fast it took Ole right along with it. Before Paul could think of what to do, Ole was out of sight.

"Come on down!" Paul yelled up at Ole.

Ole was almost beyond hearing then. When he answered, his voice took an hour to fall back to earth. "I can't come down! For every two feet I climb down, it caries me up ten!"

Paul bit the ends of his whiskers, rubbed his forehead,

and tried to think of what to do. He ordered Shotgun Gunderson to load his rifle with doughnuts and sourdough bread and shoot it up to Ole so that Ole wouldn't starve to death while waiting for Paul to rescue him.

Finally, Paul took his biggest and brightest axe and began chopping at the base of the cornstalk. The stalk was growing so fast, he couldn't hit the same place twice with his axe. He put a chain around the stalk, planning to have Babe pull the corn out by its roots. The stalk grew out over the chain and pulled it into the air before Paul could even call Babe.

Paul remembered the iron rails that the men who had been building the Great Northern Railroad had left lying beside the tracks. He marched off a few miles, picked up an armload of the rails, and came back. He tied the rails together, wrapped them around the cornstalk, and made a tight knot. The cornstalk grew fatter and thicker. With every foot the stalk grew, the iron hoop around it sank in deeper.

"It's going to kill itself if it keeps on growing," said John Inkslinger. "It's going to cut itself in two."

That is what the cornstalk did. It gave a shudder at last and started to sway. It was so tall that it took three days to hit the ground. Just before it hit, Ole jumped off, so he fell only four feet and didn't get a scratch.

The Swedish ambassador wrote to the king that the soil seemed pretty rich, and the king sent Paul a shipload of money.

Paul began looking around for an even bigger job. Most of the land nearby had been logged over, and there weren't many large forests left. Paul decided to go west to the Pacific Ocean. There were trees there so huge, called the Big Trees, that it took a day to walk round them. There were redwood trees and Douglas fir trees so tall they were bent over from pressing against the sky.

Paul told his friends good-by, and he and Babe started out for the West Coast. On the way, Paul happened to let his peavey, a pole with a sharp spike on the end, drag along behind him. This made a rut that is now called the Grand Canyon. Farther on, heading through Oregon and Washington, Babe trampled some hills in the way, and that made the passes in the Cascade Mountains.

When Paul Bunyan started lumbering in the West, the fir and redwoods began to fall like grass. He built one big camp after another and invented all sorts of ways to make the lumbering business go faster. When the biggest part of the job was done, he grew restless again. He would go and sit on a hill with the Blue Ox and think about the old days. Even though there was gray in his beard now—and gray mixed in with the blue hairs on Babe's coat—Paul felt almost as young as ever.

"We've had a good life, eh, Blue Babe?"

Babe's soft blue eyes would shine, and he would push his damp muzzle against Paul Bunyan's cheek.

"Yes, sir, Babe, old friend," said Paul on one of those starlit nights with the wind crooning in the sugar pines, "it's too good a life to leave. So I guess we'll just keep on going as long as there's a toothpick of a tree left anywhere."

Apparently, that is what Paul Bunyan and his blue ox did. They just kept on going. The last time anyone saw them they were up in Alaska. And people there say, when the wind is right, they can still hear Paul whirling his sky-bright axe and sending the shout of "T-I-M-B-E-R-R-R!" booming across the air.

Discussion

1. What would a real lumberjack be expected to do? How are these things exaggerated in Paul Bunyan?

2. Which incident do you think is the most outrageous? Why?

Coyote Cowboy

Coyote Cowboy

by Adrien Stoutenburg

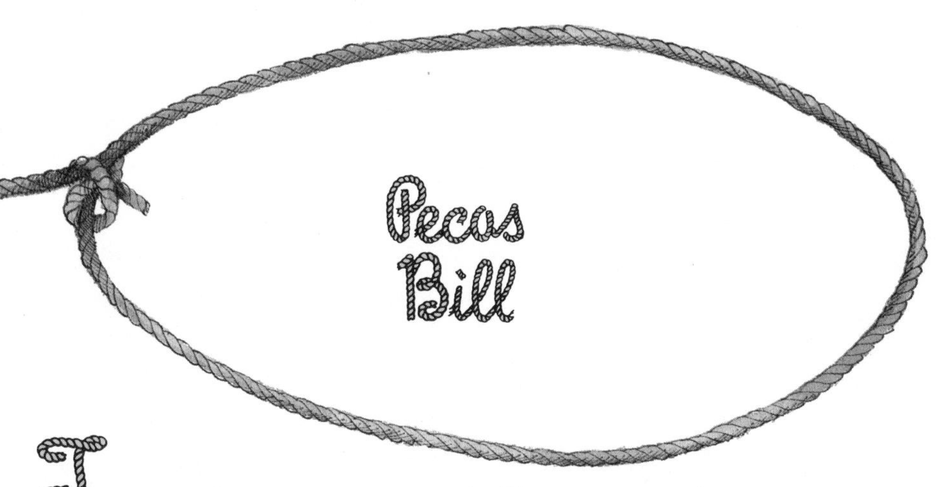

Pecos Bill

There aren't as many coyotes in Texas now as there were when Pecos Bill was born. But the ones that there are still do plenty of howling at night, sitting out under the sage-brush like thin, gray shadows, and pointing their noses at the moon.

Some of the cowboys around the Pecos River country claim that the oldest coyotes remember the time when Bill lived with them and are howling because they are lone-some for him. It's not often that coyotes have a boy grow up with them like one of their own family.

Bill was pretty unusual from the start. When he was only a few days old he raised such a fuss about having to drink ordinary milk that his mother had to go and take milk from a mountain lion who was raising baby cubs. Bill's mother was rather unusual in her own way. Before Bill was born, she drove off forty-five Indian warriors from the family's covered wagon with an old broom han-dle. So, borrowing milk from a wild mountain lion was no problem for her.

Bill had over a dozen older brothers and sisters for playmates, but they were ordinary boys and girls and no match for him. When Bill was two weeks old, his father found a half-grown bear and brought the bear home.

"You treat this bear nice, now," Bill's father said.

The bear didn't feel friendly and threatened to take a bite out of Bill. Bill wrestled the bear and tossed it around until the bear put its paws over its head and begged for mercy. Bill couldn't talk yet, but he patted the bear to show that he didn't have any hard feelings. After that, the bear followed Bill around like a big, flat-footed puppy.

Pecos Bill's father was one of the first settlers in the West. There was lots of room in Texas, with so much sky that it seemed as if there couldn't be any sky left over for the rest of the United States. There weren't many people, and it was lonesome country, especially on nights when the wind came galloping over the land, rattling the bear grass and the yucca plants and carrying the tangy smell of greasewood. However, Bill didn't feel lonely often, with all the raccoons, badgers, and jack rabbits he had for friends. Once he made the mistake of trying to pet a skunk. The skunk sprayed Bill with its strong scent. Bill's mother had to hang Bill on the clothesline for a week to let the smell blow off him.

Bill was a little over one year old when another family of pioneers moved into the country. The new family settled about fifty miles from where Bill's folks had built their homestead.

"The country's getting too crowded," said Bill's father. "We've got to move farther west."

So the family scrambled back into their big wagon and set out, the oxen puffing and snorting as they pulled the wagon toward the Pecos River. Bill was sitting in the rear of the wagon when it hit some rocks in a dry stream bed. There was a jolt, and Bill went flying out of the wagon. He landed so hard that the wind was knocked out of him and he couldn't even cry out to let his folks know. It might not have made any difference if he had, because all his brothers and sisters were making such a racket and the wagon wheels were creaking so loudly that no one could have heard him. In fact, with so many other children in the family besides Bill, it was four weeks before Bill's folks even missed him. Then, of course, it was too late to find him.

Young Bill sat there in the dry stream bed awhile, wondering what to do. Wherever he looked there was only the prairie and the sky, completely empty except for a sharp-shinned hawk floating overhead. Bill felt more lonely than he ever had in his life. Then, suddenly, he saw a pack of coyotes off in the distance, eating the remains of a dead deer. The coyotes looked at Bill, and Bill looked at them. These coyotes had never seen a human baby before, and they didn't know quite what to think. Apparently, they decided Bill was some new kind of hairless animal, for one of the female coyotes took a hunk of deer meat in her teeth and trotted over to Bill with it. She put it in front of him and stood back, waiting for him to eat it.

Bill had not eaten much raw meat before, but he knew that the female coyote meant well, and he didn't want to hurt her feelings. So he picked the meat up and began chewing. It tasted so good that he walked over and joined the other coyotes.

From that time on, Bill lived with the coyotes, going wherever they went, joining in their hunts, and even learning their language. Those years he lived with the coyotes were happy ones. He ran with them through the

moonlit nights, curled up with them in their shady dens, and howled with them when they sang to the stars.

By the time Bill was ten years old, he could out-run and out-howl any coyote in the Southwest. And since he had not seen any other human beings in all that time, he thought he was a coyote himself.

He might have gone on believing this forever if one day a cowboy hadn't come riding through the sagebrush. The cowboy stopped, stared, and rubbed his eyes, because he could scarcely believe what he saw. There in front of him stood a ten-year-old boy, as naked as a cow's hoof, wrestling with a giant grizzly bear. Nearby sat a dozen coyotes, their tongues hanging out. Before the cowboy could say, "Yipee yi-yo!" or plain "Yipee!" the boy had hugged the bear to death.

When Pecos Bill saw the cowboy, he snarled like a coyote and put his head down between his shoulders, ready to fight.

"What's your name?" the cowboy asked. "What are you doing out here?"

Since Bill didn't know anything but coyote talk, he naturally didn't understand a word.

The cowboy tossed Bill a plug of tobacco. Bill ate it and decided it tasted pretty good, so when the cowboy came up close, Bill didn't bite him.

The cowboy stayed there for three days, teaching Bill to talk like a human. Then he tried to prove to Bill that Bill wasn't a coyote.

"I must be a coyote," Bill said. "I've got fleas, haven't I? And I can howl the moon out of the sky. And I can run a deer to death."

"All Texans have got fleas and can howl," the cowboy said. "In order to be a true coyote, you have to have a bushy tail."

Bill looked around and realized for the first time that he didn't have a nice bushy, waving tail like his coyote friends. "Maybe I lost it somewhere."

"No siree," the cowboy said. "You're a human being, sure as shooting. You'd better come along with me."

Being human was a hard thing for Bill to face up to, but he realized that the cowboy must be right. He told his coyote friends good-by and thanked them for all that they had taught him. Then he straddled a mountain lion he had tamed and rode with the cowboy toward the cowboy's ranch. On the way to the ranch, a big rattlesnake reared up in front of them. The cowboy galloped off, but Bill jumped from his mount and faced the snake.

"I'll let you have the first three bites, Mister Rattler, just to be fair. Then I'm going to beat the poison out of you until you behave yourself!"

That is just what Bill did. He whipped the snake around until it stretched out like a thirty-foot rope. Bill looped the rattler-rope in one hand, got back on his lion, and caught up with the cowboy. To entertain himself, he made a loop out of the snake and tossed it over the head of an armadillo plodding along through the cactus. Next, he lassoed several Gila monsters.

"I never saw anybody do anything like that before," said the cowboy.

"That's because nobody invented the lasso before," said Pecos Bill.

Before Pecos Bill came along, cowboys didn't know much about their job. They didn't know anything about rounding up cattle, or branding them, or even about ten-gallon hats. The only way they knew to catch a steer was to hide behind a bush, lay a looped rope on the ground, and wait for the steer to step into the loop.

Pecos Bill changed all that the minute he reached the Dusty Dipper Ranch. He slid off his mountain lion and marched up to the biggest cowboy there.

"Who's the boss here?" he asked.

The man took one look at Bill's lion and at the rattlesnake rope, and said "I *was*."

Young though he was, Bill took over. At the Dusty Dipper and at other ranches, Bill taught the cowboys almost everything they know today. He invented spurs for them to wear on their boots. He taught them how to round up the cattle and drive the herds to railroad stations where they could be shipped to market. One of the finest things

Bill did was to teach the cowboys to sing cowboy songs.

Bill made himself a guitar. On a night when the moon was as reddish yellow as a ripe peach, though fifty times as large, he led some of the fellows at the ranch out to the corral and set himself down on the top rail.

"I don't want to brag," he told the cowhands, "but I learned my singing from the coyotes, and that's about the best singing there is."

He sang a tune the coyotes had taught him, and made up his own words:

"My seat is in the saddle, and my saddle's in the sky,
And I'll quit punchin' cows in the sweet by and by."

He made up many more verses and sang many other songs. When Bill was through, the roughest cowboy of all, Hardnose Hal, sat wiping tears from his eyes because of the beauty of Bill's singing. Lefty Lightning, the smallest cowboy, put his head down on his arms and wept. All the cowboys there vowed they would learn to sing and make up songs. And they did make up hundreds of songs about the lone prairie, and the Texas sky, and the wind blowing over the plains. That's why we have so many cowboy songs today.

Pecos Bill invented something else almost as useful as singing. This happened after a band of cattle rustlers came to the ranch and stole half a hundred cows.

"You boys," said Bill, "have to get something to protect

yourselves with besides your fists. I can see I'll have to think up a six-shooter."

"What's a six-shooter?" asked Bronco-Busting Bertie. (Bill had taught horses how to buck and rear so that cowboys could learn bronco-busting.)

"Why," said Bill, "that's a gun that holds six bullets."

Bill sat down in the shade of a yucca tree and figured out how to make a six-shooter. It was a useful invention, but it had its bad side. Some of the cowboys started shooting at each other. Some even went out and held up trains and stage coaches.

One of the most exciting things Bill did was to find himself the wildest, strongest, most beautiful horse that ever kicked up the Texas dust. He was a mighty, golden mustang, and even Bill couldn't outrun that horse. To catch the mustang, Bill had the cowboys rig up a huge slingshot and shoot him high over the cactus and greasewood. When Bill landed in front of the mustang, the horse was so surprised he stopped short, thrusting out his front legs stiff as rifle barrels. The mustang had been going so fast that his hoofs drove into the ground, and he was stuck. Bill leaped on the animal's back, yanked on his golden mane, and pulled him free. The mustang was so thankful for being pulled from the trap that he swung his head around and gave Pecos Bill a smacking kiss. From then on, the horse was as gentle as a soft wind in a thatch of Jimson weed.

No one else could ride him, however. Most of the cowboys who tried ended up with broken necks. That's why Bill called his mustang Widow-Maker.

Bill and Widow-Maker traveled all over the western range, starting new ranches and helping out in the long cattle drives. In stormy weather they often holed up with a band of coyotes. Bill would strum his guitar and the coyotes would sing with him.

Then came the year of the Terrible Drought. The land shriveled for lack of water, and the droves of cattle stood panting with thirst.

The cowboys and the ranch bosses from all around came to Bill, saying, "The whole country's going to dry up and blow away, Bill, unless you can figure out some way to bring us rain."

"I'm figuring," Bill told them. "But I've never tried making rain before, so I'll have to think a little."

While Bill thought, the country grew so dry it seemed that there would be nothing but bones and rocks left. Even cactus plants, which could stand a lot of dryness, began to turn brown. The pools where the cattle drank dried up and turned to cracked mud. The sun was redder than a whole tribe of painted Indians. All the snakes hid under the ground in order to keep from frying. Even the coyotes stopped howling, because their throats were too dry for them to make any sound.

Bill rode around on Widow-Maker, watching the clear, burning sky and hoping for the sight of a rain cloud. All he saw were whirls of dust, called dust devils, spinning up from the yellowing earth. Then, toward noon one day, he spied something over in Oklahoma which looked like a tall whirling tower of black bees. Widow-Maker reared up on his hind legs, his eyes rolling.

"It's just a cyclone," Pecos Bill told his horse, patting the golden neck.

But Widow-Maker was scared and began bucking around so hard that even Bill had a time staying in the saddle.

"Whoa there!" Bill commanded. "I could ride that cyclone as easy as I can ride you, the way you're carrying on."

That's when Bill had an idea. There might be rain mixed up in that cyclone tower. He nudged Widow-Maker with his spurs and yelled, "Giddap!"

What Bill planned to do was leap from his horse and grab the cyclone by the neck. But as he came near and saw how high the top of the whirling tower was, he knew he would have to do something better than that. Just as he and Widow-Maker came close enough to the cyclone to feel its hot breath, a knife of lightning streaked down into the ground. It stuck there, quivering, just long enough for Bill to reach out and grab it. As the lightning bolt whipped back up into the sky, Bill held on. When he was as high as the top of the cyclone, he jumped and landed astraddle its black, spinning shoulders.

By then, everyone in Texas, New Mexico, Arizona, and Oklahoma was watching. They saw Bill grab hold of that

cyclone's shoulders and haul them back. They saw him wrap his legs around the cyclone's belly and squeeze so hard the cyclone started to pant. Then Bill got out his lasso and slung it around the cyclone's neck. He pulled it tighter and tighter until the cyclone started to choke, spitting out rocks and dust. All the rain that was mixed up in it started to fall.

Down below, the cattle and the coyotes, the jack rabbits and the horned toads, stuck out their tongues and caught the sweet, blue, falling rain. Cowboys on the ranches and people in town ran around whooping and cheering, holding out pans and kettles to catch the raindrops.

Bill rode the cyclone across three states. By the time the cyclone reached California, it was all out of steam, and out of rain, too. It gave a big sigh, trembled weakly, and sank to earth. Bill didn't have time to jump off. He fell hard, scooping out a few thousand acres of sand and rock and leaving a big basin below sea level. That was what made Death Valley.

Bill was a greater hero than ever after that. Yet at times, he felt almost as lonely as on the day when he had bounced out of his folks' wagon and found himself sitting alone under the empty sky. Widow-Maker was good company most of the time, but Bill felt there was something missing in his life.

One day, he wandered down to the Rio Grande and stood watching the brown river flow slowly past. Suddenly, he saw a catfish as big as a whale jumping around on top of the water, its whiskers shining like broomsticks. On top of the catfish was a brown-eyed, brown-haired girl.

Somebody beside Bill exclaimed, "Look at Slue-Foot Sue ride that fish!"

Pecos Bill felt his heart thump and tingle in a way it had never done before. "That's the girl I want to marry!" he said. He waded out into the Rio Grande, poked the catfish in the nose, and carried Slue-Foot Sue to a church. "You're going to be my bride," he said.

"That's fine with me," said Sue, looking Pecos Bill over and seeing that he was the biggest, boldest, smartest cowboy who had ever happened to come along beside the Rio Grande.

That was the beginning of a very happy life for Bill. He and Sue raised a large family. All of the boys grew up to be fine cowboys, and the girls grew up to be cowgirls. The only time Bill and Sue had any trouble was when Bill wanted to adopt a batch of baby coyotes who were orphans.

"We're human beings," Sue said, "and we can't be raising a bunch of varmints."

"I was a varmint once myself," said Bill. He argued so much that Sue agreed to take the coyotes in and raise them

as members of the family. The coyotes grew to be so human that two of them were elected to the House of Representatives.

Pecos Bill grew old, as everyone and everything does in time. Even so, there wasn't a bronco he couldn't bust, or a steer he couldn't rope, or a bear he couldn't hug to death faster and better than anyone else.

No one knows, for sure, how he died, or even if he did die. Some say that he mixed barbed wire in his coffee to make it strong enough for his taste, and that the wire rusted in his stomach and poisoned him. Others say that one day he met a dude cowboy, all dressed up in fancy clothes, who didn't know the front end of a cow from the side of a boxcar. The dude asked so many silly questions about cow punching that Pecos Bill lay down in the dust and laughed himself to death.

But the cowboys back in the Pecos River country say that every once in a while, when the moon is full and puffing its white cheeks out and the wind is crooning softly through the bear grass, Pecos Bill himself comes along and sits on his haunches and sings right along with the coyotes.

Discussion

1. Which episode do you find the most hilarious? Why?

2. According to the tale, there are a few possible endings. Which one seems the most fitting? Why?

3. Do you think Pecos Bill is a good hero for a cowboy? Explain.

4. Pecos Bill is brought up by coyotes and believes he is one. Do you think such a thing could happen if a child grew up alone, only with wild animals? Why or why not?

Pecos Bill Meets Paul Bunyan

Pecos Bill Meets Paul Bunyan

by Marguerite Henry

Even though Pecos Bill was boss of all the cowhands on the ranch, and had the very finest horse in all the world to ride, and had invented roping and many new skills, he was not satisfied. He wanted to start a new ranch. A small place of just a few hundred thousand acres would do to begin with, he thought.

Whenever he had a little time to spare, he rode out on Lightning (his horse), looking for a good place to start a ranch. In those days there was plenty of acreage that anyone could own simply by claiming it. But Pecos Bill did not want just an ordinary ranch. He wanted the best ranch in all the world.

Finally in Arizona he found the very piece of land that he was looking for: grass taller than a man's head for the cattle to fatten on, creeks fed by springs of pure water for them to drink, and a few trees along the banks of the creeks for shade in the heat of the day. The land was level, except for one mountain—heavily wooded almost to its peak. Strange birds, seen nowhere else in the world, built their nests among the rocks on the upper slopes. They all laid square-shaped eggs, because round eggs would have rolled right down the mountain.

Pecos Bill thought that this land with its lone mountain would be just right for his headquarters ranch. The cattle could always roam up or down to find the climate they liked best. On cold days they could graze at the foot of the mountain; in hot weather they could move up near the top, where it would always be cool. They could even have sunshine or shade, just as they wished, for one side of the mountain would be sun-bathed while the other would be shaded. Nor would there be rain on both sides at once; the cattle could almost always keep dry unless they preferred to be rain-washed. Certainly, the wind could not blow from more than one direction at once, so the herds could always find a sheltered place.

There was just one thing wrong with the mountain. It was covered with trees, huge trees, clear up to the rocky rim. There was not room to ride a horse through the close-set trees, and certainly no room for cattle to graze there.

Pecos Bill thought and thought, but he was baffled. How could he clear the mountain of those trees? He hated to give up and admit there was anything that he could not do. Again and again he rode back to look at the mountain, trying to figure out some way to clear it for his headquarters ranch.

Then one day, imagine his surprise and anger when he found someone else on his land! A hundred men were at work at the foot of the mountain putting up a big bunkhouse and a big cookhouse. They did not look like cowboys at all, and they did not have any cattle with them—except for one huge blue-colored ox. He was a hundred times bigger than any steer Pecos Bill had ever seen before, and he had an appetite to match. He ate a whole wagonload of hay at one swallow!

Pecos Bill did not stop to think that he was only one man against a hundred men, and that the huge ox could kill a person by stepping on him. He rode right up to the camp and asked, "Who is in charge here?"

"Paul Bunyan," answered one of the men.

"I want to talk to him," said Pecos Bill.

The man called, "Paul!" And there, striding out from among the trees came the very biggest man in all the world—as big for a man as the Blue Ox for a steer. Now Pecos Bill himself was a fine figure of a man, six feet two inches high, straight as an arrow and as strong and limber as a rawhide lariat. But this Paul Bunyan was so tall that his knee was higher than Pecos Bill's head! He wore flat-heeled, broad-toed boots, not like cowboy boots at all. He wore no chaps, and instead of a leather jacket he wore a queer woolen jacket of bright-colored plaid. His eyes were deep-set and his mustaches were big as the horns on the Bighorn sheep.

If Pecos Bill was startled, he did not show it. He asked very firmly, "What are you doing on my mountain?"

"This is my mountain now," Paul Bunyan announced. "I've already settled on it."

"That makes no difference. I laid claim to this land long ago," Pecos Bill argued.

"Where's the law that says it's yours?" demanded Paul Bunyan.

"Here it is!" exclaimed Pecos Bill. "This is the law, west of the North Woods," and he slapped his hand on his pistol.

"That's not fair!" cried Paul Bunyan. "I'm not armed. In the North Woods, we don't fight with pistols. We fight with our bare fists or with our axes."

"Very well," agreed Pecos Bill. "I have no axe, but I'll use my branding iron to hit with."

Now the branding iron that Pecos Bill carried that day was known as a running iron. It was a straight bar with a crook at one end. Cowboys heated the end of the running iron and drew letters on a steer's hide as easily as you would draw with a piece of crayon on paper.

Pecos Bill heated the end of his branding iron on a blazing star that he had picked up the time the stars fell. He always carried the star with him, so as to have a fire immediately whenever he needed one.

With the hundred men watching, the fight started. Paul Bunyan picked up his axe and hit at Pecos Bill so hard that he cut a huge gash in the earth. People call it the Grand Canyon of the Colorado River.

Then Pecos Bill swung his red-hot iron, missed Paul Bunyan, and scorched red the sands of the desert. That was the beginning of the Painted Desert out in Arizona.

Again Paul Bunyan tried to hit Pecos Bill and again he hit the ground instead. The scores of strange-shaped rocks that are piled up in the Garden of the Gods in Colorado were split by Paul Bunyan's axe in that fearsome fight.

Pecos Bill's iron, instead of cooling off, grew hotter and hotter, until with one swing of his iron he charred the forests of New Mexico and Arizona. These trees, burnt into stone by the heat from Pecos Bill's running iron, are now the famed Petrified Forest.

Neither man could get the better of the other. For the first and only time Pecos Bill had met his match. And it was the first and only time that Paul Bunyan's crew had seen a man that could stand up to him.

Finally they both paused to get their breath, and Paul Bunyan suggested, "Let's sit down a minute."

"All right," agreed Pecos Bill, and they sat down on nearby rocks.

As they sat resting, Pecos Bill asked, "Stranger, why are you so anxious to take my land away from me? Isn't there plenty of other land in the West that you could have just by laying claim to it?"

"Land!" exclaimed Paul Bunyan. "It's not the land I want!"

"Then why are we fighting? What do you want?" inquired the surprised Pecos Bill.

"Why, the trees, of course," Paul Bunyan explained. "I'm no rancher. I have no use for land any longer than it takes to cut the timber. I'll log the trees off that mountain, and then I'll be through with it. I'm a lumberman."

"Why didn't you say so at first?" exclaimed Pecos Bill. "You are more than welcome to the trees! I've been trying to find some way to get them off the land so that the grass can grow on the slopes and my cattle can graze there."

"They'll be off in a few weeks," promised Paul Bunyan, and the two men shook hands.

Pecos Bill and Paul Bunyan became the best of friends after that, each respecting the other for the fight that he had put up. Pecos Bill and his cowboys delivered a herd of nice fat young steers to furnish beef for Paul Bunyan's loggers while they were clearing off the trees. When Paul Bunyan and his men were finished, they left standing their big bunkhouse and their big cookhouse and the Blue Ox's barn, ready for Pecos Bill's outfit to move in.

Roundtable Discussion

1. Compare and contrast the authors' treatment of Pecos Bill and Paul Bunyan in the tales you have read about them. How are they the same? How are they different?

2. Which tall tale do you think is the tallest? Why?

3. After all this time, why do you think tall tales still appeal to people?

4. These heroes all had animal companions. What were they? Why do you think this was so?

5. Who are the super heroes you are familiar with today? How do they compare with the ones you just read about? How are they the same? How are they different?

When Paul Bunyan Was Ill

When Paul Bunyan was ill
we sent
twelve long-stemmed sequoias.

Willie Reader

Backward Bill

Backward Bill, Backward Bill,
He lives way up on Backward Hill,
Which is really a hole in the sandy ground
(But that's a hill turned upside down).

Backward Bill's got a backward shack
With a big front porch that's built out back.
You walk through the window and look out the door
And the cellar is up on the very top floor.

Backward Bill he rides like the wind
Don't know where he's going but sees where he's been.
His spurs they go "neigh" and his horse it goes "clang,"
And his six-gun goes "gnab," it never goes "bang."

Backward Bill's got a backward pup,
They eat their supper when the sun comes up,
And he's got a wife named Backward Lil,
"She's my own true hate," says Backward Bill.

Backward Bill wears his hat on his toes
And puts on his underwear over his clothes.
And come every payday he pays his boss,
And rides off a-smilin' a-carryin' his hoss.

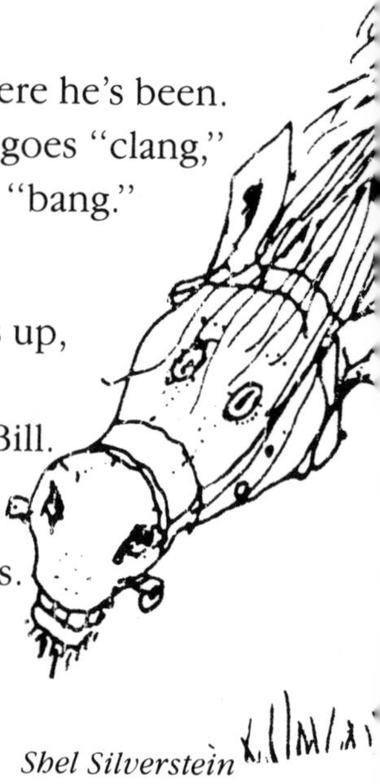

Shel Silverstein

About the Authors

Marguerite Henry Born in Wisconsin in 1902, Marguerite Henry has won many book awards and honors. After college, she began her career as a technical writer. Then she turned all of her energies to writing children's books. Her best-known books are about horses. They include *Misty of Chincoteague Bay, Justin Morgan Had a Horse*, and *The Medicine Hat Stallion*. Henry's books have been translated into German, Swedish, Danish, French, Italian, Japanese, Arabic, and other languages.

Adrien Stoutenburg Adrien Stoutenburg was born in Minnesota in 1916. She has been a librarian, a political reporter, an editor, and a writer. In addition to the stories she writes for children, Stoutenburg also writes poetry and books for adults. She has written serials and short stories for several magazines. Stoutenburg is an amateur artist, sculptor, and musician. She plays the piano, guitar, and harmonica.

Shel Silverstein Shel Silverstein was born in Chicago in 1932. During World War II, he was a correspondent for the military newspaper *Stars and Stripes*. Besides being a poet, Silverstein has also been a cartoonist, a folksinger, and a composer. Some of his songs are popular with country-western singers.

Glossary

a·cre·age (ā′ kər ĭj) *or* (ā′ krĭj) *n.* Land area measured in acres: *The acreage was cleared to make way for an amusement park.*

am·bas·sa·dor (ăm **băs′** ə dər) *n.* An official of high rank who represents his or her government in another country.

ar·ma·dil·lo (är′ mə **dĭl′** ō) *n.* A burrowing animal whose body has a bony covering that looks like armor.

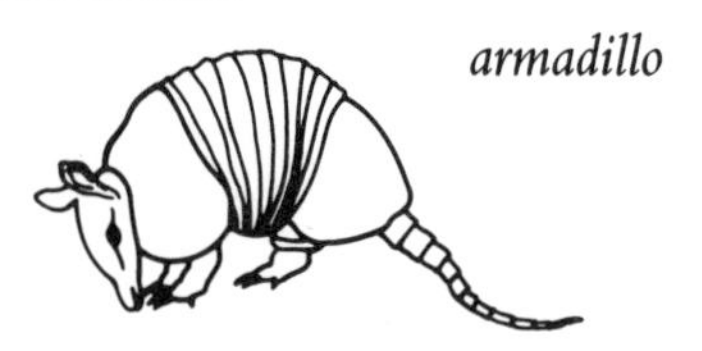
armadillo

badg·er (**băj′** ər) *n.* A burrowing animal with short legs and thick, grayish fur.

baf·fled (**băf** əld) *adj.* Puzzled; confused; frustrated by uncertainty or confusion.

chaps (chăps) *or* (shăps) *pl. n.* Heavy leather pants without a seat, worn over regular pants by cowboys to protect their legs.

char (chär) **charred** *v.* To reduce to charcoal by incomplete burning: *The fire charred the wall of the garage, leaving a blackened, shriveled surface.*

Con·sti·tu·tion (kŏn′ stĭ **tōō′** shən) *or* (**-tyōō′-**) *n.* The basic law of the United States, adopted in 1787 and put into effect in 1789.

cor·ral (kə **răl′**) *n.* A fenced-in area for keeping cattle or horses.

croon (krōōn) *v.* To sing or hum softly: *When her mother crooned a lullaby, the child fell asleep.*

drought (drout) *n.* A long period with little or no rain.

drove (drōv) *n.* A number of cattle, sheep, or other animals that are herded together.

field glass·es (**fēld′** glăs′ ĭz) *n.* A pair of binoculars for outdoor use.

field glasses

ă pat / ā pay / â care / ä father / ĕ pet / ē be / ĭ pit / ī pie / î fierce / ŏ pot / ō go / ô paw, for / oi oil / ŏŏ book / ōō boot / ou out / ŭ cut / û fur / *th* the / th thin / hw which / zh vision / ə ago, item, pencil, atom, circus

Gi·la mon·ster (**hē´** lə mŏn´ stər) *n.* A poisonous lizard of the southwestern United States, having a thick black body with pinkish or yellowish markings.

gloss·y (**glô´** sē) *or* (**glŏs´** ē) *adj.* Smooth and shiny: *The photograph had a glossy surface like a mirror.*

grease·wood (**grēs´** wŏŏd´) *n.* Any of several shrubs that grow in dry regions of North America.

grid·dle (**grĭd´** l) *n.* A flat metal surface or pan used for cooking pancakes, bacon and other foods.

haunch (hônch) *or* (hänch) *n.* The hip, buttock, and upper thigh of a person or animal: *The catcher sat back on his haunches, waiting for the pitch.*

hic·cough also **hic·cup** (**hĭk´** ŭp) *n.* A sudden catching of the breath in the throat.

House of Rep·re·sen·ta·tives (hous ûv rĕp rĭ **zĕn´** tə tĭvs) The lower branch of the United States Congress, whose members are elected every two years.

kink (kĭngk) *n.* A tight curl or sharp twist, as in a hair, wire, or rope: *The kinks and twists in the hose prevented the flow of water.*

lar·i·at (**lăr´** ē ət) *n.* A long rope with a sliding noose at one end, used especially to catch horses and cattle; a lasso.

las·so (**lăs´** ō) *or* (lă **sōō´**) *v.* To catch with a lasso—a long rope with sliding noose at one end.

muz·zle (**mŭz´** əl) *n.* The projecting nose and jaws of certain animals, such as a dog or horse.

muzzle

out·fit (**out´** fĭt´) *n.* **1.** A set of equipment needed for doing something. **2.** A group of people who work together.

pet·ri·fied (**pĕt´** rə fīd´) *adj.* Turned into stone, as wood whose structure has been replaced by minerals: *The piece of petrified wood looked like wood but felt like stone.*

sage·brush (**sāj**´ brŭsh´) *n.* A shrub that grows in the dry regions of western North America.

sap (săp) *n.* A liquid that flows through trees and other plants.

shin (shĭn) *n.* The front part of the leg below the knees and above the ankle: *The ball hit her in the shin.*

shud·der (**shŭd**´ ər) *v.* To shiver suddenly from fear or cold.

strad·dle (**străd**´ l) *n.* The act or posture of sitting astride.

team·ster (**tēm**´ stər) *n.* A person who drives a team, as of horses: *The teamsters hitched their horses to the wagons.*

var·mint (**vär**´ mənt) *n. Informal* **1.** A wild animal, especially one considered to be dangerous or a nuisance. **2.** A troublesome or despised person.

yuc·ca (**yŭk**´ ə) *n.* Any of several plants that grow in dry regions of North America, that have stiff, pointed leaves and a large cluster of white flowers.

yucca

ă pat / ā pay / â care / ä father / ĕ pet / ē be / ĭ pit / ī pie / î fierce / ŏ pot / ō go / ô paw, for / oi oil / ŏŏ book / ōō boot / ou out / ŭ cut / û fur / *th* the / th thin / hw which / zh vision / ə ago, item, pencil, atom, circus